The Adventures of Jack & Adam

The Blaze

GW00802554

Anthony Broderick

Copyright © Anthony Broderick, 2017
First Published in Ireland, in 2017, in co-operation with
Choice Publishing, Drogheda, County Louth, Republic of Ireland.
www.choicepublishing.ie

Paperback ISBN: 978-1-911131-31-1
eBook ISBN: 978-1 911131-84-7

eBook ISBN: 978-1-911131-83-0 The Larry Right Series Episode 3

A CIP catalogue record for this book is available from
the National Library.

Introduction

Book three in this enthralling new series of 'The Adventures of Jack and Adam'.

Winning isn't everything, especially when it comes to physical pursuits. Jack and Adam try to enjoy themselves at seemingly wholesome and harmless activities, but soon learn that caution needs to be exercised. There are just some arguments you cannot win outright. Along with learning the value of what they already possess, the boys soon find that it's possible for ones they love to be innocently hurt.

Chapter 1 – Setting Traps

Jack arose promptly from his bed and leaped out onto his bedroom floor to pull the curtains open. He let out a huge sigh of relief as the sun shone in, illuminating the entire room.

"Thank God!" he cried out, easing his way back from the window, stepping over several woolly jumpers and his pair of old, stained runners.

The weather had been very poor so far this summer and any sign of dryness created a certain buzz in Jack's mind. It was a buzz, however, that slightly worried Jasmine, as she knew that Jack would have to be carefully monitored when he went outside. The miserable conditions had kept the boys from getting involved in outdoor activities, but had left Jasmine with a relatively easy role of supervising the brothers from the comfort of inside the house.

Jack was usually first up these mornings. Adam was getting a little too fond of his sleep for his brother's liking. Jack called for Adam to get out of bed, as he eased his bedroom door ajar.

Adam was awake, but choosing to have another couple of minutes' rest before the third day of the summer holidays commenced.

"Come on, Adam, it's nearly nine o clock!" called Jack, still in the process of putting his jumper on over his head. Adam waved his hand up in the air to say that he wanted another two minutes to fully wake up.

"Come on, get up and look at the weather outside!" Jack said. He felt almost angry at the thought of Adam not racing down the stairs with enthusiasm.

Sure enough, within a few minutes Adam was dressed and downstairs. He was in a particularly good mood as he knew tonight was Bonfire Night.

Bonfire Night was the night in the year where people around Willows Town lit large bonfires and celebrated long into the night. Lots of people around Willows Town used this occasion to burn any waste that had accumulated during the year. Jack and Adam had been taking part in this tradition since they were young kids. They made maximum use of the day and the night, having a big party and making sure each year's fire was larger than the last, and each year's celebrating better than the year before.

Adam was wearing his favourite yellow jumper, the one that he had been given by an aunt. It was probably a little too heavy to be wearing on a day like this, but Adam was superstitious when it came to clothes, and felt this jumper brought him good fortune. He heard scratches and meows as he approached the back door to carry out his first job: feeding the animals. Club looked up all excited to see Adam making his way outside. She wagged her tail back and forth, anticipating a big meal. Adam reached for the dog bowl and poured in some dog nuts along with some of the juices left over from yesterday's dinner. He found it amusing watching Club eat her breakfast; it was as if she was just swallowing it all down, without taking any time to enjoy the taste.

"What would they do without you?" chuckled Mum. She raced about, hanging clothes on the line, aware that she had to be in work at half nine.

After Adam had taken care of Club he went back inside to fetch a tin of cat food.

"Meow, meowwwww!!" Diamond called. She looked annoyed that she hadn't been fed first.

Adam had the press well stocked with Diamond's favourite, chicken and beef cat chunks. He peeled back the silver tin cover and tipped out all the nice chunks of meat onto the top of the recycling bin. Instantly Diamond sunk her teeth into the cold meat, while Club pawed at the recycling bin to try and get some seconds. Adam really did love seeing the animals happy. Any pocket money he received from doing odd jobs here and there was spent on one of the two. He had once spent fifteen euro on purchasing Club a warm rug to keep her warm during the cold nights in her shed. Unfortunately the rug did not last too long, as Club began using it as a toy and soon shredded it into little bits of fluff. He walked inside to wash his hands before getting ready to eat his own breakfast.

Dad had already set off for work. He was only working a half-day today as he was taking his two weeks' annual summer holidays. The boys had noticed the enthusiasm in their Dad's demeanour in the last few days. Each morning he would be heard whistling to music on the radio as he placed slices of ham into some brown loaf for his lunch. Mum too was on her last day before her annual leave, so soon all four would be able to go on outings or maybe take a few days away at the beach if the weather stayed fine. Jack and Adam liked it when their parents were off, but it had its disadvantages. They would not be able to pull the wool over Mum and Dad's eyes, as they could so often do with Jasmine, and jobs like doing the dishes and hanging out the clothes would no doubt become more frequent.

"Right, Jasmine is here. I'll be home later, make sure there's no trouble," said Mum. She grabbed her keys and let Jasmine in through the front door.

Jasmine entered the kitchen as punctual as ever. She was dressed very summery with her dark blue sunglasses and light blue pants.

The boys greeted Jasmine in unison, wishing her a good morning as they slurped down the cold milk at the bottom of their cereal bowls.

"Ok, let's go," said Jack. He beckoned Adam to follow him down to the treehouse to make plans.

Jack could see Club and Diamond on top of the summer bench that Dad had brought up from the shed a couple of days ago. The animals loved resting on top of this bench as they had a good view of the kitchen window. They could see if Jack or Adam were going to come out, and felt important being high off the ground. Club looked like the king of the jungle she lay majestically down. The only problem was the warp that was gradually developing towards the centre of the bench as a result of how heavy she was.

Adam slowly walked out, pulling the edges of his runners up behind his heels. All four met up at the treehouse to discuss their plan for the morning. Even though dog and cat could not technically engage in conversation, they were considered valuable members of the team.

Jack stretched his neck to look over to the far side of Granny's house. There was a massive heap of old timber, wooden desks, some cut grass, three decrepit chairs and lots of others bits of scrap, all resting in one big heap. It was where the big fire would be taking place later that evening. Jack smiled, admiring the work he and his brother had done yesterday, gathering all of these things together, and looked forward to his Dad lighting it all up in the evening. Some of the neighbours, other family members, and two of Jack's good friends from school were all set on coming over to enjoy the party.

"Should we gather more stuff to burn?" asked Jack. He scanned the perimeter for anything that he could add to the pile.

"Dad said that was plenty yesterday. The fire will be big enough," replied Adam sensibly.

"Right, let's make some traps to protect our area here so," said Jack. He flew down the treehouse stairs.

He and Adam had come up with the idea of setting up traps around their territory during the last few days, after watching a gripping episode of *The Larry Right Hour*. In the episode Larry had designed some booby traps as a practical joke on some of his friends, which had worked very effectively. Jack had similar ideas of carrying out some practical jokes on Jasmine or any other friends that might pop over. He knew that the traps would also act as a security measure around the treehouse in case any unexpected visitors decided to gate-crash their meetings.

Jack glanced around the area for anything useful.

Adam felt that they should try to create the Tyre Trap first, so he made his way to the back of the shed to see if there were any old tyres to use. Sure enough, he found four. They had to be heaved up from the heavy clay and grass, as they had probably been lying there for the past three or four years. Next Jack organised a small piece of rope, which he intended to tie onto a solid piece of wood at the top of the treehouse stairs. Adam carefully rolled the tyres up to the top of the steps while Jack fed the rope through the middle of the four tyres to hold them in place. It was quite a difficult task for the boys, as Club thought Adam was playing a game and kept getting in the way. He had to keep throwing down her red ball to get her out of the way. She was shedding more and more hair at this time of year so the fluff that blew onto

Adam did not help.

The tyres were heavier than expected so a good tight knot was needed to prevent them from rolling down.

"Brilliant!" cried Jack. "This will come in very useful if someone tries to climb up the steps."

All the boys needed to do now was cut the rope and the tyres would go flying down the steps at top speed.

"Looking good!" said Adam. He smiled as he took a little step back to observe their creation.

"Come on, now for the second trap!" Jack called, not wanting to waste any time. He jumped over the tyres, down the stairs onto the fresh-cut grass.

Next they planned on digging a medium-sized hole beside the treehouse. The intention was to create a sort of pit which could be covered over with a blanket, and then some leaves and soil would be placed on the top to blend it in with the rest of the environment. If someone walked across it they would go plummeting down into the ground.

"Ha-ha! This should be fun if Jasmine comes down to call us in for dinner!" sniggered Jack.

He began using his foot to step on the shovel to give it that extra bit of force, slicing through the ground.

Diamond got engrossed in playing a little game with some of the beetles and creepy-crawlies as they rose to the surface. She placed her white paw in front of the dashing insects as they tried to find some soft clay to dive back under. Jack dug and dug until the hole was up to his hip level. He jumped in, clearing out the loose clay with his hands.

Adam decided to transport all of the clay and grass behind the back of the shed so it would not look obvious that they had just dug a hole. The more digging and moving of clay the better for Club, as she adored getting herself as dirty as possible. Sniffing around and rolling in the clay was when she was at her finest. She began to look more like a black Labrador than a white one.

As Adam emptied the clay onto a heap, he noticed an old carpet slightly sunken into the ground. He grabbed the corner of it and lowered himself down to the ground for support. He pulled and tugged until the carpet rose up and was visible. It was quite damp and heavy and had a terrible smell of rot. It was dark red in colour and looked to have been a little burnt in a fire of some sort some time ago, to judge by the dark black patches around the edges. Club instantly went for her usual sniff around to inspect what she was dealing with.

"This will be great to use for the top of the pit!" Adam thought aloud to himself as he hauled it back towards his hard-working brother still down in the hole. "We can use this, Jack!" he said. He proudly lifted up one side of the carpet to show his brother. "This won't sink down, and we can cover it over with some leaves and grass."

"Good man, well spotted," Jack replied.

Adam grabbed a smaller shovel and hopped down to give Jack a hand with the digging. The deeper they went, the more difficult it was to remove the clay, but neither Jack nor Adam were going to settle for a hole less than shoulder-level.

Adam made several more trips back and forth with the clay and soil until finally the pit was deep enough. Jack patted the sides of the hole to prevent the earth from crumbling in, and then pulled himself out.

They covered the hole with the carpet and got several large, leafy branches to camouflage the carpet's colour and blend it into the rest of the area.

"One more thing. I think you'll like this little effect," hissed Jack, making his way to the back of the treehouse.

He lifted over a large bucket which appeared quite heavy, then placed it on one of the carpet's edges.

"What's that?" asked Adam. He hardly dared to ask.

Jack flicked back the lid of the bucket gently and pointed inside. "This is over a gallon of tar. I found it in the shed last week, and I knew it would come in handy."

Adam stuck the top of his shovel into the jar for an inspection and sure enough, it was pitch-black and very sticky. He realised that placing this on the carpet's edge meant that whoever stood on the carpet would not only fall deep into the pit, but also have black tar fall over them.

Diamond strolled along the carpet, brushing by the bucket. She was light enough to walk over it, but Jack and Adam had to make sure Club kept well away. She would definitely go plop, straight down the hole, not to mention getting destroyed in tar.

The boys looked forward to showing Dad the traps when he came home early from work in the afternoon, but as for Mum, they felt that showing her would probably be a bad idea. Still, they felt really great about their morning's work, and walked up to the house for a much-needed and well-deserved drink of water.

Chapter 2 – The Foiled Surprise

"What are you two up to down there?" Jasmine inquired. "Why are your hands filthy?" She met the boys as they stepped inside.

"Just relaxing and enjoying the weather," replied Jack. He winked at Adam.

"Your parents were telling me that you both are going to the sports day later on, so make sure you don't give them any reason for giving out!" said Jasmine. She slid the back door shut to prevent Club or Diamond coming in also.

"*Sports day*? We didn't know about this!" Adam and Jack shouted. They looked at each other in a mixture of confusion and excitement.

Jasmine stood upright, tilting her head to the brothers and realising she had made a blunder.

"Oh… sugar! Maybe it was a surprise, maybe I shouldn't have said anything," she said, feeling stupid.

"Great!" Jack called out. "We'd better get prepared."

Being the boy he was, the sports day was now Jack's main priority; everything else that was going on was put aside. Both Adam and Jack loved sports, but the thought of a competition always made Adam nervous. The tension that kept building up in his gut stopped him from achieving his goals. Images of himself competing during PE lessons, with teachers shouting at him, came surfacing back into his mind.

From their previous experience of sports days, there was always the egg-and-spoon race, the sack race, the three-legged race, but most important was the sprint. This was the race they felt they had an edge over boys and girls of their age, as they were exceptionally quick and always competed against one other at home. Sometimes, as a challenge, Adam would hold Club until Jack got a head-start, then see how fast he was at getting away. Nobody wanted to be jumped on and dragged down from behind by a heavy-breathing, slightly overweight Labrador, so the boys would run as fast as they could to escape from their dog. Also, the fact that they spent quite a lot of time outside meant that they had a good level of fitness. Jack was always top of his age group at school and Adam was almost the number one. One boy, called Richie, would always just pip him at the finish line, but this motivated Adam to keep trying to beat him some day.

"Right, let's go out and do some stretches for later on!" said Jack, full of energy. "We'll start off with some light jogs and then we'll do a few fast sprints," he explained, deciding on the area of grass to use.

Adam followed his brother outside once again and tried to compose himself, not wanting the butterflies in his stomach to get the better of him. Diamond was stretched out as usual on top of the bench, without a care in the world. That's the attitude I need to try and develop, thought Adam, glancing over to the relaxed feline.

First the boys tied their laces tightly and began with some leg and arm stretches to loosen up their limbs before some light jogging on the spot. When the running commenced Club got involved as the team mascot, dashing around in all directions not really knowing what was

going on.

"We'd better eat some bananas as well, Jack," said Adam, deciding to go back in and grab one or two from the fruit bowl. As he did so, he was greeted by Mum and Dad, who were obviously home a little early.

"I see you found out about our little surprise," cried Dad, eyeing Mum at the table. Jasmine felt even guiltier now; she knew she had spoilt the surprise.

"Right, well, I have the picnic made and packed from last night, so let's go when everyone is ready!" Mum called out. She got up from the table and walked down to her room to put on some shorts and a cool T-shirt.

The brothers got changed into more comfortable running clothes. As much as Adam wanted to wear his lucky jumper, it wasn't suitable to run in during the heat of the afternoon. Jack put on his old runners that had colourful laces. They had always done well for him since he bought them in the shop at the bottom of Willows Town.

Dad soon appeared from his room wearing his summery red shorts. The boys knew it was summer when Dad wore these shorts, as it was rarer than seeing a four-leaf clover. Dad seemed to be in a great mood, humming a few tunes and clicking his fingers to the beat. He walked over to the kitchen press and reached inside for the two flasks. Tea was an essential part of everyday life for Dad. It didn't matter whether it was thirty degrees outside; a flask of tea with precisely two spoons of sugar was in order to keep him on top form. He poured the boiled water into the shiny inside layer of the two thermal flasks. Adam watched as the smell of tea permeated the kitchen. Diamond, who probably wouldn't even drink tea, looked in through the window, intrigued.

"Grab the rug from under the stairs!" Dad then instructed Adam, who had moved up close behind him.

Adam advanced down the hallway and opened the wooden door under the high stairs, searching about for the rug. All sorts of items had just been thrown into this room. Mum had always done her best to keep it clean and organised but Adam could not help his old habits of tossing things in and shutting the door, not wanting to even look at the mess. As expected, under the ironing board was the old rug that the family had always used for picnics or going to the beach. Adam only needed to take one look at this rug and memories of summer would flash into his mind. He could even remember right back when he was only a two-year-old boy, sitting on his Dad's lap holding onto this rug with one hand, as he clutched a warm bottle of milk with the other. He had come a long way since the age of two, and for a brief moment wondered what life would be like for him in another eight years.

This moment of nostalgia was interrupted, however, when Dad began ordering everyone in the house to meet at the car inside two minutes. Adam threw the cosy black rug over his back and raced into the toilet to get a dash of sun cream to protect his fair skin on this scorcher of a day.

Chapter 3 – Hammer Time

The family met as scheduled, by the car, all looking very animated about the prospects of what this sports day could offer. Both children and parents had a chance to have a bit of fun and meet loads of new people.

"Here you go!" Jack said, holding out a medium-sized egg and a large spoon towards Adam for the race.

"Thanks," Adam replied, happy that his brother had not forgotten about him and had chosen a sturdy egg for the competition. Adam placed it in his bag and rolled down the back window a little for the air.

Dad drove out the gate singing his famous 'It's Summer Time' tune, which in one sense Adam and Jack enjoyed because it was nice to see their Dad having a good time, but on the other hand they were glad they were in the car to protect them from embarrassment. Dad drove the red car, which he had owned for the last five years, up through Willows Town, passing Mr and Mrs Pegs' shop. The roads up through Willows Town were badly maintained and many people in the village – even 'The Wanderer', who did not even own a bike, never mind a car – were often heard complaining about the local council and the state of the roads. The family passed by the Willows Inn and Mrs Slate's butcher shop, and went on up to the football pitch, where they could see hundreds of people beginning to gather.

"Wow, there are a lot of people already here!" said Dad. He glanced back towards his two sons to see if they were as excited as he was.

Adam, whose stomach had become more settled during the drive, now felt a cold sweat beginning to seep out of his skin, as he saw all the commotion around one of the goalposts on the pitch. He reached for his bottle of water to moisten his drying mouth and took several deep breaths.

Mr Pegs was at the entrance to the pitch collecting a five-euro fee.

"Good afternoon, Mr Pegs," said Dad, pulling the window down a little to hand over the money.

"Great day, isn't it?" Mr Pegs replied, handing over a yellow ticket as proof of payment.

Dad parked the car beside several others along the upper bank of the pitch.

As Jack hopped out of the car he flinched a little in the sharp glare of the sun. "You were right to bring sunglasses," he said. He looked over to Mum, who looked like some high-roller poker player from Vegas with her pitch-black shades on. Mum pushed the glasses tightly behind her ears, feeling very important and posh.

"We forgot to bring the sack for the sack race," said Jack. He faced his brother and kicked the ground in disgust.

"It's okay, we can just do the sprinting and egg-and-spoon race. That will be fine!" Adam answered. He did not really want to take part in every activity anyway, and just wanted the sprinting to go well.

"I might go over here for a quick look," said Dad. He had noticed some stalls that were set up along the pitch. He took particular notice of a group of sturdy-looking men gathering around an open stall.

Dad pushed the car door shut and clipped his keys to the hook on his shorts. As he walked slowly over he became more and more curious. The boys followed suit, intrigued by the characters that this first stall was attracting. Loud masculine cheering echoed throughout the area.

"One, two, three, four, five, six, seven!" a plump man behind the stall called out in a deep voice, before a clatter of chanting filled the air.

As the boys and their father approached they realised that it was some form of hammer-and-nail event that the middle-aged men were engaging in. Most of the men looked very robust and seemed to have dominant personalities to suit, to judge by the way they carried themselves and shouted loudly. They eyed up Dad closely as he approached. Dad, who now realised Adam and Jack had followed him, kept the boys close as he eased his way towards the counter.

"Would you like to have a go?" asked the stall-holder. He grinned from ear to ear, looking Dad up and down. He had red hair and a very noticeable handlebar moustache. "You just have to sink this nail into the wood in as few hits as possible," he explained, pulling one of the long six-inch nails out from a cardboard packet.

As the chanting died down, several of the other men who were hanging around the stall began sniggering to themselves and whispering to each other. They glanced over at Dad, who was considerably smaller and lighter than the rest of them. By now Adam had lost all his anxiety about the sprints, and could feel a little anger building up in his belly, as he did not like his Dad to be insulted and looked down upon.

Jack, on the other hand, knew very well that Dad was no amateur when it came to hammering nails into wood, as he did it practically every day at work, so this challenge should be interesting.

"Yes, I would like a go," Dad called out in a confident voice. He stretched out his right arm to get some elbow room at the counter.

The man looked very surprised, but he quickly offered the hammer and nail to Dad, still wearing a sarcastic grin on his face.

"Five euro is the entry fee," he said, holding out his hand as if it was a guaranteed five euro for his pocket.

Dad reached into his shorts and pulled out a nice fresh five-euro note. It looked so fresh Adam knew it had probably come out of an ATM as part of some summer bonus from work. More middle-aged men closed in, and whispers began flying.

"The record is six taps to sink the nail clean into the wood," explained the stall man. He winked at another observer to the side. Adam caught a glimpse of this individual, who was by far the largest man he had ever seen. He had a striking brown beard and puffed cigarette smoke out from between his gritted teeth. He had his sleeves pulled up, revealing arms and wrists like tree trunks, and there was a cheeky smirk on his face. Right beside him was another, smaller, skinny-looking man who appeared to be stuck to him. He also sniggered in the direction of Dad while glancing up at the larger man every few seconds. Adam realised this large man was probably the record-holder for this event, as he carried himself like a cocky champ, while the other measly individual was probably one of his followers.

Dad gently wiped his palms across his summer shirt to get a dry grip on the hammer's handle. He then aligned the large nail with the wood. He gave one quick glance at Jack and Adam, who now had free front-row seats to watch the spectacle.

*Bang!*went the first tap, slicing a large deep hole in the old wood. He was off to a good start. A large crowd had now gathered, and new onlookers craned their heads over the shoulders of those closest.

*Bang!*went the second tap, and again the nail sank cleanly and deeply into the slightly knotted timber. Adam could see the focus in his Dad's eyes as he aligned the hammer with the nail for his third blow.

*Bang!*went the third tap, which was definitely the most crucial. Dad was within a single tap of sinking this nail 'home and dry' and becoming the new record-holder. The largest man to the side now began to come closer, his smirk changing to a frown, as the others took notice of him coming through. Dad noticed this in the corner of his eyes as he gave it everything,

sinking the final inch of the long nail into the wood.

Suddenly a large roar overwhelmed the stall area, a mixture of surprise and confusion. Dad had done it; he had defied all odds and beaten the record. The stall owner could not believe his eyes as he examined the head of the nail carefully to make sure it was fully sunk.

Adam noticed the large man making his way to Dad. His scrawny sidekick kept by his side, looking like a young kid keeping with his Mum for fear he would get lost. The big man held out his shovel-sized right hand and congratulated Dad with a firm handshake. Adam noted a sense of respect in this man's voice which slightly confused him. He expected some of the onlookers, especially this man, to be a little bitter at the fact that this random smaller man had come into their territory and taken first prize. But ironically enough the man appeared to be quite humble after all.

"Thank you," Dad replied. He flexed his fingers and tried to contain his emotions, but he was ecstatic inside.

The stall owner then held out a cheque for fifty

euro and put out his hand to shake Dad's.

"Wow! Fifty euro!" Adam called out. "That's brilliant!"

"We'll head to the shop," Jack suggested, smiling back at his brother.

Dad placed his arms around the two boys and headed back to the car, where Mum still was. As the boys walked either side of their Dad they felt very proud.

Chapter 4 – The Sprint

Mum had organised an area of grass where she was setting up the family's picnic just in front of the car. Lots of other families were preparing picnics nearby and children ran about enjoying their time off. The sun was still very intense, and along with her sunglasses Mum now wore a straw hat on her head. She noticed how happy the boys and their father all looked as they approached, stretching out the rug to create a square on the grass.

The boys couldn't wait to recount what had just happened. Jack gushed with laughter and excitement as he sat down and got comfortable on the rug. As the three family members shared the latest events, Adam stood up, stretching and squeezing his eyes together on account of the sharp midday sun. Scanning the area, he noticed a familiar figure in the distance, and squinted a little just to make sure he wasn't seeing things. His stomach turned. Sure enough, that was Mr

Atkinson organising some event on the pitch.

"What is he doing here?" Adam thought aloud, trying not to think of school during the summer holidays. "Mr Atkinson is here!" he shouted.

Jack was in the middle of telling the now-famous story to Mum, but that got his attention. "What?" he said, turning around in shock. "What's he doing here? You would think he would be abroad on holidays somewhere."

"I think he's organising the sprints," said Dad. He stood upright to get a closer look.

The picnic was postponed for the time being and all four made their way over to the crowds of people. As Adam approached he noticed Mr Atkinson was wearing a white shirt. He hoped that this meant he would be in a good mood, just like when he wore his white shirt at school. He wore his usual glasses and had a pair of rather skimpy summery shorts on. He had a clipboard and paper in his hand and his usual PE whistle hung around his thick neck. Lots and lots of young boys and girls hovered around the area, eagerly awaiting the start of their race.

"Girls under-fourteens!" announced Mr Atkinson, as children scampered into position.

He then blew his whistle to deal with the hustle and bustle of the crowds emerging.

Adam and Jack recognised some of the children who were gathering. Adam spotted a girl called Amanda, who lived just outside Willows Town. He discretely pointed her out to Jack, not wanting her to think they were staring at her. She was by far the most beautiful girl in all of Willows Town, and every kid wanted to be friends with her.

Jack surmised that she was probably very good at running, as well as other sporting events, gazing at her blonde hair, which still looked good even though it was tied up in a bun.

"On your marks, get set and GO!" Mr Atkinson shouted and all participants set off, with members of the crowd roaring at the tops of their voices for support.

Several of the girls set off quickly in the lead, and in the distance the boys could see Amanda way out in front. Soon she sped through the yellow ribbon at the end of the sprint track, slightly bumping into some of the supporters surrounding the finishing area. A big cheer went up as she held her arms in the air in celebration.

Someone the boys did not recognise was taking the names of the participants and noting the results at the finishing line. He was carrying a little pouch strapped around his waist, which presumably held the medals. Jack expressed a keen desire to win one of the medals as he bent down to make sure his socks, shorts and laces were properly secure.

"Boys under-twelves next!" Mr Atkinson cried out. He identified Adam and Jack among the runners.

"You are up, boys!" said Dad excitedly. He patted the two on their backs simultaneously. Then he took up his usual position to the side, where each year he would practically run the race himself from outside the ropes.

Mum had now come upon the scene and winked at Adam as he got himself focused. Both brothers would be in the same race together this year, along with what looked to be about twelve others. Among the twelve Adam spotted his arch-rival, Richie, who had taken a central position at the starting line. Adam felt that nauseous, tense feeling gripping his stomach as he lined up, awaiting the signal to go. Jack positioned himself just a little up from Adam and had that familiar focus on his face. Mr Atkinson glanced over to make sure all runners were behind the starting line before beginning the countdown.

"On your marks, get set and GO!"

Adam shot out of his marks like a greyhound chasing a rabbit. The worry and doubt in his stomach vanished as that "GO!" sound surged through the cells in his brain, telling his legs to run. The uproar of the crowd was deafening but the only sounds the two boys could hear were their minds telling them "faster, faster". Dad was sprinting sideways up the course, shouting on at the top of his voice, his keys clattering against his exposed thighs.

Jack gave it everything, surging over the finishing line in second place. Adam was just behind, ducking his head down to claim that all-important position ahead of Richie in third place.

Dad raced around to congratulate the two boys on their great achievement. Mum too scampered around to enjoy the moment, eyeing the tall boy who had just claimed first prize.

As Adam panted and panted, trying to regain his breath, he forced himself up to shake the hand of the winner. "Well done!" he said.

"Thank you!" the boy replied, seemingly unfazed by the challenging sprint he had just won.

Before Adam could get a chance to chat to the boy, he darted off in the direction of another event. Adam looked around to shake Richie's hand but he too had vanished from the scene. This was the first time Adam had beaten Richie and it was a milestone in his sprinting career. He felt as if he had achieved something great. He hoped Mr Atkinson had gotten a good look.

Adam and Jack collected their respectable second and third prize medals from one of the stewards. It was still roasting hot on the pitch and Adam could feel the sun cream dripping off him in the sweat released in the race.

"Let's go back to the picnic and get some drinks!" said Mum. She was looking forward to relaxing for a while now. She took the two medals from the boys lest they lost them.

"Good idea," responded Jack, remembering that

Mum had packed two chocolate cakes into the picnic bag earlier.

Chapter 5 – Fight Fire with Fire

Dad had packed several multi-coloured plastic containers to act as mugs for the hot tea. The family adored the tea that Dad made, as it always seemed to taste much better and gave them that all-important boost of energy that they needed. While slurping back some of the tea Adam stared over at Mr Atkinson, who was still trying to get each race under way. For a brief moment, it made Adam see a more honest and unselfish side to his teacher. He was giving up his free time to help out at this sports day, leaving his young child, with whom he could be spending time with at home. As Adam emerged from his brief daydream, Jack stood up, crumbs of sandwiches and cake at the corners of his mouth. He grabbed his and his brother's eggs and spoons and proceeded to walk out onto the pitch again.

"Come on, Adam, we have to do this race, seeing as we did pick out two very good eggs," said Jack, still swallowing some pieces of food.

Adam slurped down his tea and took the egg and spoon from his brother. He giggled to himself as he examined the egg; it looked more like a flat rubber ball than something that had been produced by a hen.

"Ha! I don't know where you found these, Jack, but they are genius!" he replied. He placed the egg and spoon in his right hand, all ready for the race.

"Good luck, lads! Head back over here after, and we'll set off home to prepare for the bonfire," said Dad. He reached for the bottle of sun cream to apply a top-up.

"Yes, the barbeque and bonfire! I knew we had forgotten about something," replied Adam enthusiastically.

"We'll be back after we bag another few medals," said Jack. He dashed over across the field.

Only four other children seemed to be taking part in this activity, besides Adam and Jack. Oddly enough, they were the only boys. It was four girls who greeted the Willows Town brothers as they took their positions behind the starting line.

"Hi, boys!" the girls screamed simultaneously, all excited and giggly.

Jack and Adam stood red-faced and speechless. It was a moment where they really wanted to say something confident back but those words just wouldn't quite roll out.

All the girls wore bright red shorts and white T-shirts. Their eggs did not look as aerodynamic as Adam and Jack's, but the girls did look quite fit and nimble.

"And GO!" shouted the steward, blowing his air horn to signal the start of the race.

The noise of the horn came as a bit of a shock to the boys, wobbling them a little from the get-go. Gradually they both got into the routine they had practised so often, except this time they did not have an overweight white Labrador tailing them. They soon advanced into an overwhelming lead over the girls, hearing amused giggling in the background as the girls dropped their eggs over and over again. Adam and Jack practically walked over the winning line, this time finishing in a tie.

As the finishing rope fell down in front of them,

they couldn't help looking around again at these four girls who were only half way through the course. The boys had just won the race but those four girls were having more fun than either of them. They stared at each other for a brief moment, not saying anything but both thinking along the same lines. Maybe sports days are not all about winning. The group of girls stumbled over the end line minutes later and straight away rushed up to the boys in ecstasy.

"Whoop! Whoop! Well done!" they chanted, while Jack and Adam nodded shyly. The girls gathered up their eggs and spoons and slipped off to another event.

The brothers strolled back across the crowded pitch to the car feeling relatively pleased. They now had one more medal in each of their pockets to add to the success of the day. The highlight, however, had to be Dad's win in the hammer-and-nail event. This would leave unforgettable memories in the boys' minds.

As Jack reflected on his second place in the sprints his mind drifted towards the bonfire, which would soon be up and running. He relished summer days when lots of activities were packed into one day. This is what he lived for.

"We should stop at Ibrahim's on the way home," said Adam, feeling he needed an ice cream to get a boost for the big evening ahead.

"Ya, good call," replied Jack.

Then he came to an abrupt stop. Looking ahead, he saw Dad throwing his hands up in the air in anger.

As Adam came closer, he could see the right front tyre of his Dad's car was completely squashed. The car was tilted to one side.

"How did this happen?" roared Dad, visibly in distress. "The tyre has been slashed!"

Jack bent down on his hunkers. He inspected the tyre, which now looked more like a flat pancake. He raised his head and scanned the area suspiciously. Adam joined his brother to investigate and he could see from the rip in the tyre that it had obviously been tampered with. It had been clearly targeted.

Then the boys caught sight of their Dad. He was staring over at the man who had congratulated him for winning the hammer event earlier, at whose side stood his weasel-like partner, giggling. They both leaned against the bonnet of a jeep, staring at Dad and sneering.

The boys realised what had happened. Mum too. She moved over towards Dad, advising him not to do anything he would regret; just change the tyre and head home.

Adam knew his Dad was fuming. Those jealous men had deliberately done this. He could see his Dad's day had been ruined because of it. It wasn't fair.

Adam shot another angry look over at the men, then called his brother over and whispered, "Mum might not be allowing Dad to do anything about this, but we won't let them get away with it... I have an idea."

Jack was fully on board. He listened to his brother as he explained his plan, his smile becoming wider as he began to understand what his brother was saying.

While Dad began changing the tyre, Adam described to his brother that they would fight fire with fire. If these men wanted to damage their Dad's car, then their jeep would feel the brothers' wrath.

Adam pointed out a few things, and Jack knew

exactly what to do. He casually walked over to a cluster of trees. He jumped up on a bit of the tree stump and broke off a thick branch. Crouching down, he returned towards his Dad's car. Adam stood out in the open, diverting some attention, as his brother snuck across an area of grass to the back of the men's jeep. He turned his head left and right to make sure nobody was walking by or looking in his direction.

He then placed the thick stick into one of the jeep's alloy wheels.

He and his brother knew that if a branch or a stick was placed between the spokes of a bicycle wheel, it had a good chance of damaging it as it turned. Jack tweaked the stick until it went in one part of the alloy and out of another. Meanwhile Adam kicked some stones onto the field to keep the attention of the men.

Jack kept low and snuck away from the jeep. He smiled at his brother as he made his way over to his Dad to help with the tyre change. Adam winked cheekily and waved at the two men before joining the others.

Later, as Dad drove angrily out of the gate, forgetting to wave to Mr Pegs, who had a tired look on his face, Jack and Adam looked out the back window, knowing they would have the last laugh.

Mum knew that continuing with the plan of the day was the best remedy. She was always the positive one and never liked reflecting on the bad things that happened, and preferred it if everyone got on and moved on. The family stopped at Ibrahim's for a much needed ice-cream.

Ibrahim, a man from Pakistan, ran the only chipper in Willows Town. He had a great way with the customers. His son Omar whom the boys knew from school, helped him manage a very efficient service directly across from the Willows Inn pub. Regular visitors to the chipper received extra chips and even sometimes a portion of chicken nuggets free of charge. Ibrahim always had time for locals, greeting Dad with a big handshake as he and the rest of the family sauntered in.

"How are you all on this beautiful day?" asked

Ibrahim, offering high fives to Jack and Adam.

"We're good!" replied Jack, connecting well with the palm of Ibrahim's hand.

Adam placed his two arms up on top of the high counter and examined the ice cream menu.

"Can we get four large strawberry ice creams please?" Dad ordered, knowing what the boys' favourite was.

Adam and Jack smiled at each other, realising that Dad was back in a good mood and also feeling that he might be on a little spending spree.

Town was quite busy on the way home with many families and couples out walking and relaxing. Lots of elderly men gathered outside the Willows Inn on account of an important football match that was being televised. Loud roars were to be heard as supporters watched every kick of the ball with eager attention. The sun still lit up the streets and the men, women and children were out in their colourful outfits. Jack even spotted 'The Wanderer' sitting on a deckchair with a pint of beer in front of him. He still wore his usual raggedy suit pants and shirt but now he was also wearing a cap on top of his head.

"Everyone seems to be having a good day," said Mum. She squinted a little due to the glare through the windscreen.

Jack rolled down his side window and stuck his head out for some fresh air. Upon doing so he thought he could see the weasel-like man from earlier pacing back and forth on the path. As Jack turned to try and see more he noticed a cloud of cigarette smoke billowing up into the sky, and then saw a man throw his cigarette angrily down on the ground.

It was the large brown-bearded man.

Then he looked up and caught Jack's eye. Jack immediately pulled his head back through the window. He bit into the strawberry at the end of his ice cream, wondering if the man had identified him.

When Dad drove into the driveway, Club was heard moaning from the distance.

"We're home, Club!" Adam cried out, jogging down to open the back wooden gate.

Club was about to jump all over Adam and lick his hands until she spotted the ice cream in his hand. She sat back respectfully, eyes bulging, anticipating a scoop. She knew that if she acted like a mad dog she would not get any food. Adam took one large mouthful and then threw the rest of the container onto the ground. It had hardly touched the hot tarmac before Club had snatched it in her mouth. She held it in her teeth and went off to a more shaded area, where Diamond lay, to enjoy the mini meal in comfort.

Dad had not been in the house two minutes before he was out again, this time wearing his pair of old jeans and a torn shirt from work. He also wore a pair of disposable plastic gloves, which fitted tightly around his fingers.

"When you are ready, give me some help to gather more stuff for the bonfire!" he said. He pointed his hand towards Granny's shed.

Chapter 6 - Dad's Bonfire

Jack zoomed out the door wearing a different T-shirt, with a pair of disposable gloves on his hands too. He encouraged Adam to follow him, explaining that there was a lot more work to get done. He ran through the far gate with Club galloping behind.

Adam eased his way in through the back door, stepping aside to allow Mum to carry some of the picnic accessories through. He walked up the stairs to his room and pulled out some really old clothes from his wardrobe.

He followed his father and brother over towards Granny's shed. The shed was quite small in comparison to their turf shed but it was home to a variety of items to be disposed of. Old chairs and cupboards were piled untidily on top of some of the turf from previous years. Jack and Adam had recently helped their Dad make a few new presses for Granny's kitchen and the remains of the old pieces had just been thrown in here. Diamond strolled in at this point and took up a front-row seat on top of a pillar to watch the action.

All three had to be very careful lifting the furniture, as nails often stuck out dangerously. They pulled out as many useless items from the old shed as possible, then brought them around to the back of the shed and set them beside the large heap already accumulated there.

Adam lifted one end of a large kitchen table while his brother helped with the other side.

They lifted it up high on the pile ready to be burnt. As Adam made his way back again for another load he came to a stop.

"Whoa! What's that?" he said. He stood still, his eyes fixed towards something yellowish hanging down from the shed's window ledge. It was oval in shape and looked like it had little holes or pores all over it. He pointed ahead, to where he could hear gentle yet fearful vibrations coming from some sort of nest. There seemed to be little things crawling and hovering all around it.

"What type of nest is that?" said Adam. He

frowned as he went a little closer to inspect.

"That's no bird's nest anyway… that's a nest… with wasps," responded Jack. "Look at the shape of it!"

"What? Keep back," whispered Adam, hearing the word "wasps" and now noticing more and more of the yellow insects crawling out the front hole of the nest.

"This is perfect," whispered Jack. He raced into the shed and came back out with a large shovel.

Adam kept moving, not wanting to disturb the wasps, and continued to help his Dad gather more stuff to burn. Gradually the area piled up with more and more rubbish. Adam laughed to himself as he even threw in an old football that had been destroyed from use.

"We sure are making use of this fire!" he chuckled.

"Yes, but look at Club, she's taken more stuff away," replied Dad. His eyes followed the dog as she strolled away with something grasped between her teeth. She was once again proving more of a pest than a help in preparing the bonfire, as each item the boys threw on top of the heap she tried to grab and bring off to her own corner to chew on.

"She's preparing her own little bonfire for the evening," laughed Adam, as he watched his Dad lift a large stone up off the ground. Dad was taking some safety precautions before any fire was started. He was placing stones around the perimeter of the bonfire to prevent the fire from spreading. He had also left several sheets of galvanise to the side in case the fire needed to be slowed down.

Jack suddenly arrived back on the scene. He had been away for several minutes, and Adam wondered where he had been.

"Hey, Jack, go in and get some of the stools in our house," said Dad, noticing that there was nowhere for anyone to sit down.

Jack darted back across to his own house and brought back ten wooden stools in three trips. He placed them back from the bonfire for people to sit on during the evening. He made sure to place a nice comfortable cushion on a stool intended for Granny, as she was an important figure in this annual event. Each year she would tell stories of her past and lots of the neighbours and friends would chat and laugh amongst each other late into the night. Jack thoroughly enjoyed the sweets and chocolate he and his friends were allowed feast on as they sat by the heat playing games of cards and enjoying the banter.

"Hey, guys, I hope we haven't missed much!" said a voice from the distance.

"Wow, you've gathered so many things!" said another voice, this one softer.

Jack and Adam looked up to see who it was. Two people came running down the grass with bags of sweets in their hands and dressed in shorts and T-shirts. It was Paul from school and his sister Tina.

"Oh hey, I forgot it was that time already," said Adam, greeting the two and inspecting the sweets to see what types they had brought. Tina darted straight over to Club and patted her up and down. Club rolled over on the grass and stuck her tongue out, loving the attention.

"Some of my friends are coming over later as well, they're going to bring lots more food for the party," said Tina, all excited. She took some of the sticks and cardboard that Club had stolen and threw them high up on the pile.

"Right, it's time to light this up!" Dad shouted, feeling very eager. He stood back to make sure everything was ready. He then reached into his trouser pocket and took out a box of matches and some paper. He lit a match carefully and then placed the flame next to some dry pieces of cut-up envelopes that he had found in one of the old drawers. Dad was very smart when it came to starting fires and knew all the tricks to make sure it would ignite quickly.

He gradually added more pieces of paper and some cardboard, and soon some chunks of wood to the growing flames. Large bright flames now took the place of the mouldering grey smoke that lingered from the paper-burning.

Mum was still in the main house getting burgers and sausages ready for the barbeque. She had bought the food in Mrs Slate's butcher shop and all the family knew that they were in for a treat. The boys could hear lots of chatter coming from their own house, which more than likely meant that many more of Jack and Adam's friends and neighbours had arrived.

Club and Diamond were now enjoying the heat

from the bonfire. They occupied a nice flat area just away from the burning timber. The few cattle in the nearby field had trotted over, putting their solid heads over the fence, their eyes fixed on the flames. Club cocked her ears; she had heard a door open nearby. Granny appeared wearing her black skirt and cardigan. In her hands were many packets of biscuits.

"God bless the work!" she called out, patting Diamond on her head. She waved around at everyone before sitting down on her stool.

"I'll bring over some tables so we can line up all the food and drinks," said Tina. "I think Paula and Marisa have arrived as well. I'll bring them all over," she added.

"The heat… It's getting so hot!" commented Adam as he poked at some of the burning timber.

It really was a beautiful spectacle seeing the distinct orange flames rising up, with waves of heat blurring the vision. Watching the timber singe and burn was so relaxing; it was almost like therapy for the mind.

"Right, I'm going to help Tina bring over the tables and see how the food is doing. Keep an eye on that fire and don't put anything else in for a while," said Dad. He flicked off his disposable gloves and headed over with Granny and Paul to his own house.

The aroma of the cooking burgers and sausages had now blown out towards the bonfire and it was delicious. Club noticed Dad walking over and used this as an excuse to try and get some of the food before it was portioned out. She lifted her nose into the air and galloped over.

"We'll keep an eye on this!" said Jack, still full from the big ice cream and fascinated with the large bonfire that was now in full flame. He also knew that Mark and Liam, his close friends from school, would be here any minute and he really wanted the bonfire to look as good as possible.

Adam decided to wait with his brother bending down to stroke Diamond's warm skin.

"Let's see if there's any more stuff in the shed for burning later on," said Jack. He knew there was much more rubbish in the shed if they had a thorough look. Adam followed him back into the shed, where they scanned the area for anything else their Dad would like them to get rid of.

"What about this plastic stuff here?" Jack said, pointing towards a square piece of foam covered with white plastic.

"That's part of the shower tray that we took out of the bathroom last year," Adam replied. He began lifting up the timber and turf surrounding it and pulled it out from beneath a pile of sticks.

"Dad will definitely want to get rid of this. It's only taking up room in this shed," said Jack. He helped Adam drag it out onto the grass and around to the back of the bonfire. "We might as well throw it in now, and when we come back it will have burned," added Jack, gesturing at Adam to fling it up.

The two boys grabbed either side of the tray and, on the count of three, heaved it up on top of the burning rubbish. As it landed on top it caused a lot of loose burnt paper to rise up and some smoke to form like a cloud.

Adam commented on how large the heap was by now, feeling a little surge of adrenaline building up in his body. Jack stood further back now on account of the intense heat.

Chapter 7 – Out of Control

Within moments a *crack* was heard: the tray split in half and was swarmed by vicious, onrushing flames. Adam and Jack could see the insides of the tray. It seemed to be composed of some sort of yellow foam. Both boys now had to stand back even further, and watched a pall of pitch-black smoke spreading over the evening sky. The smoke grew thicker and the heat more intense, and before long the boys had a feeling of unease.

"This isn't right!" cried Adam, who knew now that they should not have thrown the tray in the fire. "Oh no!" he shouted, "It's going to burn the telephone wire."

The fire had now gotten out of control; even though it wasn't spreading outwards it was towering far too high in the sky, up towards the main electricity supply wire.

"Quickly, we need to stop this!" said Adam in a panic, not knowing how to go about doing it, as the heat was so hot now it was burning the hairs on his hands.

Jack paced from side to side, trying his best to think fast and do something. But what could he do?

Crack! Another sound the boys feared to hear; now a piece from the shower tray had fallen out over the bonfire's edge and onto the dry grass surrounding it.

It instantly began to spread, leaving a trail of black smoke. The pace at which it was taking over territory was frightening. Jack had a look on his face that really worried Adam. It was a look of intense fear. He was in such a state of panic that his body was trembling.

Mum and Dad, who had noticed the unusually thick smoke, came racing over, soon followed by many of the other guests.

"What happened?" Dad shouted, his eyes wide with shock. "Quickly, grab those sheets of galvanise!" he roared, pushing Adam on the shoulder to make him act fast.

Jack, realising his Dad was in a frantic state, snapped out of his shock and sharply turned, looking for sheets of galvanise. Adam scampered over with him and dragged a large rectangular sheet towards the scorching blaze. Normally they would not have been able to lift such a large sheet but they did not have time to think about its weight and just used every muscle in their body to carry it out.

Dad threw the sheet up onto the bonfire, where it held back some of the towering flames. The wave of heat from the fire swept across the boys' faces as they stood back, the black smoke now filling the air.

But the fire began to spread even further. The flames dashed around another area of grass and attacked some of the pots of vegetables that Dad had planted during the year. The flames from the bonfire had found a way around the sheet of galvanise and now rose up again towards the electric wire.

Adam coughed and coughed as he helped his Dad shove another large sheet on the very top.

"Another one!" Dad ordered, running over to drag a third out.

The boys lifted two smaller sheets by themselves and used all their might to toss them up onto the sides of the bonfire, their faces

reddened with the heat. Adam could barely open his eyes for the black smoke. Jack was finding it difficult to breathe.

As the galvanise carried out its role of eliminating oxygen from the fire, the smoke gradually lessened and the air cleared for a brief moment. Mum, with the help of some friends and neighbours, had filled a large barrel with water and now tipped it over onto the scorching grass. A singeing sound festered through the air and lighter smoke billowed up.

Diamond gazed at the spectacle from the top of a fence, confused as to whether this was some sort of game or some sort of crisis. Dad inspected the garden to make sure that every last flame had been dealt with. The nearby grass had been devastated, and now appeared more like a desert on account of its black colour. Jack coughed and coughed as he eased his way back onto a rock to sit down. His clothes, like Adam's, had been ruined and his face and neck felt like they were on fire.

Dad gave a sharp look over at the boys, who were too ashamed to even look up. Jack caught a glimpse of his friends Mark and Liam standing nearby, carrying large boxes of crisps and bottles of fizzy orange, unaware of the danger of what was happening. Mum blessed herself again and again as she sat down for a moment's rest after the trauma.

Just as everything seemed under control, a lingering moaning sound filled the air. It sounded like an animal in pain. At once Adam looked up to scan the area for Club and Diamond. The shock of what had just happened faded out of his mind as he listened attentively for another moaning sound.

Dad rushed over to an area of grass that had escaped the fire. "Oh no, Club, what happened?" Dad cried out softly, bending down to examine her.

Adam and Jack feared the worst. They raced over, in a panic, hardly daring to look.

Club was lying flat on the ground and bleeding heavily. Her stomach was raw and tender.

"She must have got burned by something," Dad exclaimed, rubbing her head to show that he and the boys were here to help her.

Adam's heart pounded. He was afraid even to

look at his pride and joy in agony on the ground.

"We'll have to bring her to a vet immediately," cried Mum. She knew that, as with the fire, they needed to act fast.

Dad rushed back to the house to get a large cloth to wrap around the exposed cut and burn. Adam helped Jack carry Club towards the car, both trying their best to be gentle.

Some of the others had now realised what had happened, and went up to the dog. Tina took one look at Club and immediately turned her head away, unable to cope with what she could see. Liam and Paul dropped their bags of food to the ground and stroked Club's head. Diamond crawled in among the people and went right up to Club's face, sensing something was terribly wrong.

"Okay, we have to go!" shouted Dad. He got people to move away so he and the boys could put Club in the back of the car. "We'll be back in no time. Clean up things here and keep the fire going." Dad didn't want the night's fun to finish, and winked at Mum and Granny to try and get back to the celebrations while they were gone.

Club's dark eyes looked up at the boys and Diamond in distress.

"It's okay, Club, it's okay, we'll get you help. Hang in there," Adam said, with tears in his eyes.

Adam and Jack both kept Club comfortable in the back seat of the car, rubbing her and hugging her to keep her warm. The cloth was slowing the flow of blood but unfortunately it wasn't stopping.

Dad had rung a vet who lived on the outskirts of Willows Town. The vet's name was Vinny. He was relatively new qualified and based in Beach Heaven. He was meeting the family halfway, as this was clearly an emergency. Dad was smart enough to leave the car's flashers on so Vinny would recognise them on the road and not pass them by.

"That car is slowing down up ahead," said Jack.

"That must be him," Dad replied. He pulled the car over to the side of the road.

"Vinny, thanks very much for coming," Dad said quickly, opening the back door of the car to let him examine Club.

Vinny was wearing ordinary clothes and didn't look at all like a typical vet. He carried a little briefcase with him and had a stethoscope hung around his neck.

"Okay guys, let's take a look."

He popped his head in the back door and looked closely at the wound. He put on a pair of disposable gloves and gently lifted Club's eyelids up to examine her pupils. Club had lost quite a lot of blood at this stage and was visibly weakened and fatigued.

"Okay, she has suffered a bad burn, presumably from something like a hot coal that fell out of the fire. She will need some surgery right away," explained Vinny. He tried his best to sound positive in front of the two boys, who stood looking worried outside the car. Adam turned away as Vinny reached for a syringe from his briefcase.

"Do what you have to do," answered Dad, squinting his eyes a little to hold back his own tears.

"We're coming with you," the boys said.

They helped Vinny place Club on a mini stretcher and put her into the back of his blue van. Inside it smelled just like a hospital, a smell that neither the boys nor their father relished. Adam kept stroking his favourite pet, praying she would be okay. Everyone knew that the sooner Vinny could operate and heal this open wound, the better the outcome would be.

The drive to Vinny's surgery felt like one of the longest journeys Adam had ever known. Negative thoughts kept crowding into his mind and created a constant pain in his gut. Jack was regretting ever topping up the fire and knew he might have made one mistake too many.

In the surgery Vinny gently laid Club out. He took out a long needle and explained to Dad that he was just going to put the dog to sleep using a general anaesthetic.

"Will she be okay?" Adam asked, flinching at the sight of the needle.

"Yes, she should be," Vinny replied. He shaved some of the hairs on Club's paw to locate the correct area to inject the anaesthetic. Within moments her eyelids closed and she was asleep.

"You will have to wait here," said Vinny, pointing to the waiting room, as he wheeled Club into another room to carry out the procedure.

"Can I talk to you for one moment?"

Vinny gestured to Dad, who followed him into the next room.

Through the doorway, Jack and Adam could see Vinny standing next to Dad and whispering something in his ear. They looked at each other, wondering what he might be saying.

When Dad walked over to sit down beside the boys, Adam quickly asked him what Vinny had said. Dad responded positively, saying that he was told the operation might leave Club a little weak for a few days and that they would have to take good care of her.

"I definitely will," said Jack, who was now feeling regretful that he didn't always give Club the attention that she deserved.

Dad's mobile rang. It was Mum wondering how everything was going. She explained that Diamond was not her usual self and seemed to sense that something bad had happened to her companion. She also pointed out that the whole night was not lost, as a smaller bonfire was now burning, and friends and neighbours were eating, chatting and having a laugh.

"We'll be home soon," said Dad, ending the call. He watched the surgery door, hoping Vinny would come out shortly.

After one dreary hour, the door of the vet's surgery opened. Vinny wheeled out a stretcher and pulled a mask from around his nose and mouth. He was dressed in his white cloak and still had the stethoscope fastened around his neck. He paused and scanned all the anxious faces in the waiting room. His face widened as he smiled to the two boys.

"She is a little groggy, but she is okay," said Vinny. He then walked away and allowed the boys and their Dad to say hello to the patient.

It was as if a huge weight had been lifted from their shoulders. Loud, relieved breaths filled the air.

"Oh thank God, I knew you were strong!" Adam cried out, carefully rubbing Club's soft head up and down.

Her tail slowly moved as if to say hello back. She looked tired and very delicate after her operation.

"She will have to stay here overnight so I can monitor her and also she will have to wear this," said Vinny. He held up what looked like a lampshade and placed it over her head. "She needs to wear this to prevent her from licking out some of her stitches when they get itchy." He positioned the lampshade around the dog's head and made sure it was comfortable. "It will only be for a while until it heals. Your dog has been very lucky. There have been lots of dogs locally that have been injured over the last few weeks and unfortunately some haven't made it," added Vinny.

Dad nodded his head and thanked Vinny once again before paying him for his work. Club was then wheeled back in through the surgery door.

They all hated to leave poor Club here overnight but knew she was in good hands. The hard part was over, and in the morning the boys could collect her. As Adam sat inside the car he thought about how he could have lost his partner tonight because of some silly carry-on during the bonfire. He also reflected on how earlier in the day they had taken justice into their own hands by sabotaging the man's jeep. He wondered whether it was karma.

Jack, on the other hand, just kept still and silent

for the journey home. It was as if he was turning something over and over in his head.

Chapter 8 – Rendezvous

"I don't feel like joining the others. I might just go to bed," said Adam as he arrived home, hearing chatter and laughter from next door.

"That's okay, I'm going inside anyway to let your mother know about everything," responded Dad.

"Hey, Adam, follow me for a minute, I need to tell ya something," said Jack. He tipped his brother on the shoulder and began walking down the back of the house. Adam slowly followed, and Diamond joined them, walking along the wall.

"What is it?" asked Adam curiously.

"I've been thinking. Ya know how Vinny said earlier that a lot of dogs as of late have been brought in injured and that? Well, what if the Woodsman is back?!" Jack threw a look at his brother.

"What?" said Adam.

"Fredrick Potter – what if he's back?"

Adam stood, tired and confused.

"The police have been looking for him for nearly a year now. Maybe he hasn't moved at all and is still down in the cottage. When we went down again that time, remember that crack? I knew we should have checked it out," whispered Jack.

"I don't know. I've had enough of an adventure today, I can't handle any more," answered Adam with a sigh. He turned to head up to the house.

"Okay, okay, we'll check that out again. But just come over to see the gang before bed, they'll be looking for ya," said Jack eagerly.

Adam stopped and listened over the wall. It did sound like everyone was having a great time and lots were his friends, after all. He decided he should head over for a quick word.

As Adam and Jack walked through the gate, followed by Diamond, they noticed the majority of the gang gathered around two deckchairs facing away from them. Adam was confused, as neither he nor his brother had pulled any of these fancy chairs out, and he wondered who was sitting on them and what they were doing that was so interesting. The fire had calmed down considerably and lots of empty packets of biscuits and sweets lay on the grass. Granny was nowhere to be found; now all that were out were Jack and Adam's friends.

As the boys came closer, they noticed two large hands resting either side of one of the chairs.

"Adam! Jack! Hey guys, how's Club?" shouted Tina. She looked wound up and was chewing something very fast in her mouth. "Why didn't you tell us your Dad's friends were coming over? They've been telling us all about winning the hammer-and-nail event and how you fixed their jeep. They're so fun!" exclaimed Tina.

"Ya, it's been brilliant," added Paul.

Jack and Adam looked at each other. They were very puzzled. What friends were they on about? As they got closer to the deckchairs they could see more of who was in them. Jack breathed in and out heavily, trying to think who it could be. Suddenly one of the people began to get up, revealing thick brown hair. Adam could see a pair of large rough hands, then two square shoulders and a thick neck. Then the man turned his head as the other person sprang out of the chair and turned around. Jack and Adam jumped back in fright.

Adam's heart skipped a beat. All tiredness vanished from his body. He and his brother stood face to face with the two men from earlier: the large man and his smaller, weasel-like buddy.

"Hey guys, this has been such a great party and your friends were telling me your poor dog got injured. How is that poor little doggy?" asked the larger man in a condescending tone. The other guy sniggered as he drank back a bottle of lemonade.

Jack and Adam looked at each other and began to run. They ran as fast as they could all the way back over to their property and straight up into the treehouse. Jack jumped over the tyre trap and shut the door behind his brother, then peered out of the window.

"How did they find us?" said Adam, panicking.

"I thought one of them saw me earlier on the way home. Damn it, I bet he followed us!" responded Jack. He slid across to the other side window to see if anyone was coming.

Within moments he saw the two men

approaching, gazing around the garden in search of the boys. They lifted up some large blue barrels and looked inside. Jack could now see the larger man's partner from a distance. He really was a measly looking individual. He wore a tattered top and had a horrible crooked nose. He seemed to be doing most of the searching while the bigger man just casually walked around.

"Where are they now?" hissed Adam. He was afraid to look out in case he was seen.

"He's looking under the bushes, he's going to look down here soon, I can feel it," answered Jack. He looked back and forth in distress. He then grabbed a pair of scissors that they kept inside the treehouse.

Adam now looked into Jack's eyes and could tell by where Jack was looking that the men were close to their treehouse. He flicked his eyes around to see if there was anything else he could defend himself with, but there was nothing. He then tapped the sides of his pockets and felt something hard. He realised that the medal that he won earlier was inside.

The larger man now stroked his beard and

beckoned his sidekick towards the treehouse. He had noticed it wasn't that high up off the ground.

"Get up and check in there," the big man ordered. He waved his hand to tell the other guy to head up the stairs and check it out.

Adam and Jack both heard this from inside and their pulses pounded in their necks. Jack kept his head out of sight and peered out through a small hole in the wood. Adam clung onto the sides of his top, almost feeling the man's presence.

"I think I see someone," screeched the skinny man, peering through one of the treehouse windows.

As he stepped up the stairs Jack jumped up and leaned out of the window with the scissors in his hand. He cut the ropes in two clean cuts, releasing the tyres, which fell towards the man. Adam heard the bounce of the tyres as they hit the man's scrawny body. The force pushed him down into a prickly rose bush at the bottom of the stairs. He let out a shout as a thorn sank deep into his skin.

Now Adam moved out from behind the door

and stared out the other window to see what was happening. His heart was beating faster than he could bear.

"I'll get you!" shrieked the weasel-faced man. He pulled some thorns out from his top and started to walk up the stairs towards Jack and Adam again. Adam was clenching the medal in his hand.

"Wait!" ordered the larger man, now coming to a halt. He held his hands up in the air to tell the other man stop what he was doing. He looked over to the side of the treehouse where there was something grabbing his attention.

"Leave them, Sal. Let's get this one," said the large man. He pointed towards the ground. "I heard your poor dog had a little bit of an accident earlier on… It's a shame your other pet is going to have a little accident as well," he said, sniggering.

Jack stretched his head out the window and saw Diamond casually strolling along the grass and suddenly come to a stop. He now realised what the man was talking about. He was going to get Diamond.

"No!" shouted Jack, stretching his head out

farther to try and get Diamond to run. Adam also realised what was going on and shouted her name over and over to get her to flee. But Diamond just sat still and licked her paws.

Sal jumped off the stairs and smiled back to his boss. "Good thinking, sir," he whispered.

The two of them held their hands out and open and slowly moved in Diamond's direction. The larger man wore a threatening look on his face and Adam knew he was going to hurt her badly. He needed to do something.

"Go, Diamond, go!" Adam shouted. He threw the treehouse door open.

The men were closing in slowly, holding their breath so they wouldn't scare her away.

"Stop!" shouted Adam once again.

He threw the medal in his hand out towards the cat. Diamond immediately lifted her head from her paws and noticed the two strange men. She leaped up in the air and dashed towards the treehouse.

Seeing this, the two men rushed towards her. Diamond sprinted away. The scrawny man raced forward, but suddenly his right foot disappeared, his body fell forward and down and his chin hit the ground with a thump

It took a moment for Adam to realise what had happened: the man had stepped on the carpet fallen into their trap! Adam flinched as he saw the bucket wobble, then spill its load of tar on top of him.

The larger man couldn't stop himself. His momentum took him down into the pit and he collapsed onto his sidekick. Adam heard two shouts of pain and confusion – one high-pitched, one low. Then, for a moment, there was silence.

Seconds later Adam heard a low vibrating sound, followed quickly by screams and screeches. The two men's heads popped back up out of the pit, then ducked down and up and back and forth. Then the large man raised his arms and scrabbled around, trying to pull himself out of the pit, pushing his sidekick out of the way.

He appeared in a rare state of agony. The other man's head now appeared, covered in tar, as he tried to pull himself up onto the grass. They were pulling and scratching at all parts of their bodies, as if they were being bitten.

Jack jumped down out of the treehouse to see what was happening. He heard the vibrating sound and knew exactly what it was. He could now see about a hundred very mad wasps attacking the two men from head to toe, as some of them stuck to the tar and were stinging the men viciously over and over again.

The large man now pushed Sal to the side and pulled himself up along the grass to try and escape, still screeching out loud. Sal grabbed onto the man's leg and was pulled up out of the hole, his weasel face black with the thick tar. The two men ran for their lives, with the wasps following them up the garden and out onto the road.

Jack and Adam stood still, watching it all, as Diamond walked up to them and curled up between Adam's feet. They continued to stand and stare as the men moved out of sight.

Then Adam dropped to his knees in exhaustion. He looked at Jack, understanding what had happened. Jack smiled. He had transported that wasp nest and positioned it on the carpet as another accessory to the pit trap. It had worked perfectly.

There was a few moments' pause.

"Ah well, another one bites the dust," said Jack. He bent down and stroked Diamond from side to side. "Great work, Diamond. You lured those men nicely into the drop zone. Absolute genius!" he added.

Adam smiled thinly with the corner of his mouth, although he felt like anything but smiling. What a day it had been! What he and his brother had done throughout the day had created a great deal of trouble. He thought about how he could have lost not only one of his pets and partners, but two. He also wondered whether or not it would be the last time he saw those men.

The End

Books in *'The Adventures of Jack and Adam'* series

For more information on 'The adventures of Jack and Adam' series, please visit us on www.jackandadamadventures.com

Also by Anthony Broderick
'The Larry Right' Series

eBooks now available in the Larry Right series

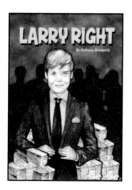  

For more information, please visit us on
www.jackandadamadventures.com